Anna [illegible] & Christopher Weyant

Will You Help Me Fall Asleep?

THE
FROGATTA
BOAT RACES
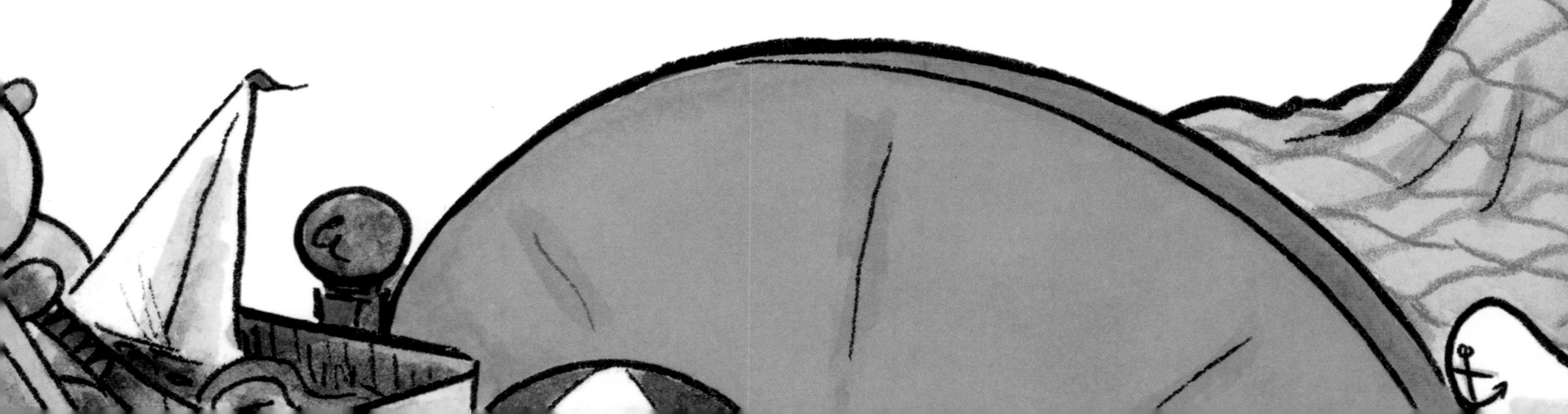

Hi! I’m so glad you’re
here. I need your help.

I've been lying here
for hours and nothing
is happening.

NOTHING!

I can't sleep!

I am

WIDE AWAKE!

And do you know what else?
I'm going to be in big, big trouble.

Because if I don't get a good night's sleep . . .

. . . my mum won't let me go to the boat races tomorrow!

And my mum always knows if I don't get a good night's sleep. I don't know how she knows, but she does.

I.
AM.
NOT.
TIRED!!!
BUZZIES

I race my boat every year. All my friends will be there. I just *have* to go to the boat races!

What's that? SLEEP?? I told you, I'm trying but I can't!

Ohhh, did you say ‘sheep’? Like *counting* sheep? OK, I’ll try . . .

7
46
BAAAAA!!!
124
BAAAA

BAAAAA!!!
12
2
AAAA!!!
49
6

Sheep scare me a little.
They're so . . .
BAAAA!
. . . LOUD.

Any other ideas?
A book?
I love
books!
Good idea!
SHARKS!
POP-UP

AAAAHH!!
SPROING!
SHARKS!
POP-UP

Maybe later.

It’s really dark . . . and quiet.

I don’t like dark and quiet.

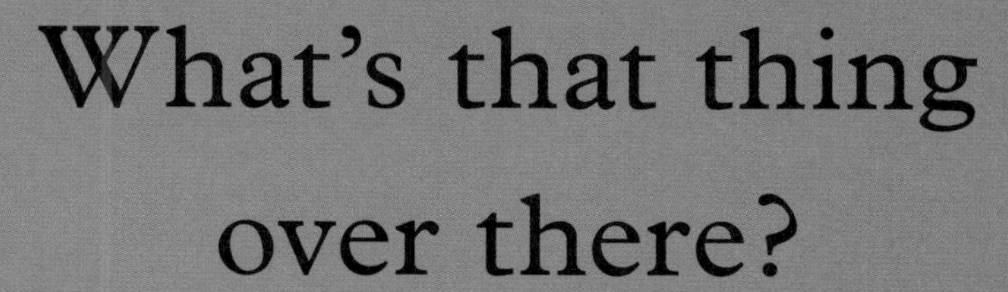
What's that thing
over there?

Ohhh,
it's Mr Dimple!

I won Mr Dimple
at the boat races
last year.

Monty? Who are you talking to?
Go to sleep!
OK, Mum!

But I can't.

When I get sad at school
Miss Chon tells me to take
a slow, deep breath.

She says to go to my 'happy place'.

ICE CREAM
YAWN!

I love the boat races . . .

Last year I finished in tenth place . . .

Some kids cried . . . Not me . . .

I was happy . . .

That was such a good day . . .

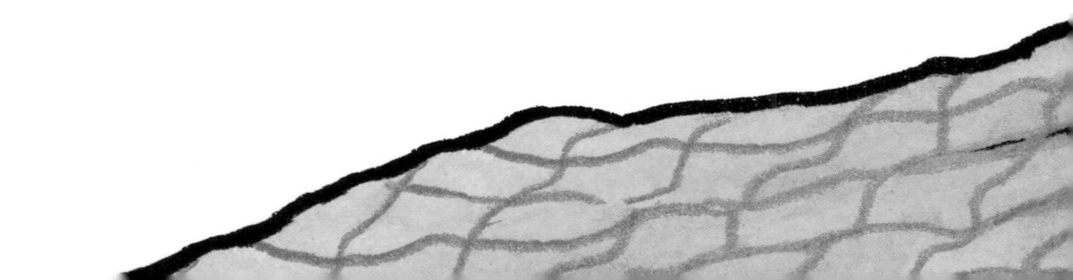

Thanks for your help
and for being . . .
my . . .
friend . . .
Goodnight . . .

To children everywhere,

may you have sweet dreams.

With love, Anna & Chris

HODDER CHILDREN'S BOOKS

This edition published in Great Britain in 2019 by Hodder and Stoughton.
Originally published by HarperCollins, Inc. 2018
Used with the permission of Pippin Properties, Inc. through Rights People, London

A CIP catalogue record of this book
is available from the British Library.

HB ISBN: 978 1 444 92644 6
PB ISBN: 978 1 444 92646 0

1 3 5 7 9 10 8 6 4 2

Printed and bound in China.

MIX
Paper from
responsible sources
FSC® C104740

Hodder Children's Books
An imprint of
Hachette Children's Group
Part of Hodder and Stoughton
Carmelite House
50 Victoria Embankment
London EC4Y 0DZ

An Hachette UK Company
www.hachette.co.uk

www.hachettechildrens.co.uk